For Viktor Christen

LADIES & GENTLEMEN!

I SEE A SONG. I PAINT MUSIC. I HEAR COLOR.
I TOUCH THE RAINBOW, AND THE DEEP SPRING IN THE GROU
MY MUSIC TALKS. MY COLORS DANCE.
COME, LISTEN, AND LET YOUR IMAGINATION
SEE YOUR OWN SONG.

I SEE A SONG

by Eric Carle

SCHOLASTIC INC.
New York Toronto London Auckland Sydney

ISBN 0-590-25213-5

Copyright © 1973 by Eric Carle.
All rights reserved. Published by Scholastic Inc.
BLUE RIBBON is a registered trademark of Scholastic Inc.

12 11 10 9 8 7 6 5 4   8 9/9 0/0

Printed in the U.S.A.   08

First Scholastic printing, January 1995

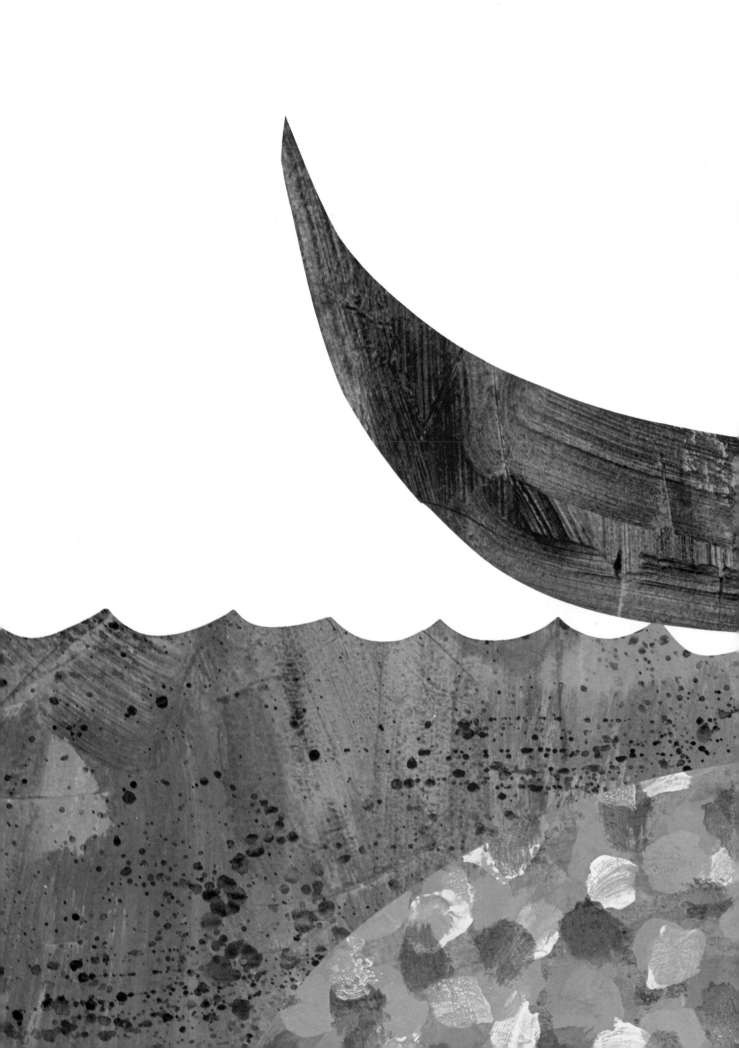